THE FIRST AND FINAL VOYAGE
THE SINKING OF THE TITANIC

BY STEPHANIE PETERS
ILLUSTRATED BY JON PROCTOR

Librarian Reviewer
Laurie K. Holland
Media Specialist (National Board Certified), Edina, MN
MA in Elementary Education, Minnesota State University, Mankato

Reading Consultant
Elizabeth Stedem
Educator/Consultant, Co
MA in Elementary Education,

D0006524

STONE ARCH BOOKS
Minneapolis   San Diego

Graphic Flash is published by Stone Arch Books,
A Capstone Imprint
151 Good Counsel Drive, P.O. Box 669
Mankato, Minnesota 56002
www.capstonepub.com

Library of Congress Cataloging-in-Publication Data
Peters, Stephanie True, 1965–
    The First and Final Voyage: The Sinking of the *Titanic* / by Stephanie Peters;
illustrated by Jon Proctor.
    p. cm. — (Graphic Flash)
    ISBN 978-1-4342-0444-8 (library binding)
    ISBN 978-1-4342-0494-3 (paperback)
    1. Graphic novels. I. Proctor, Jon. II. Title.
PN6727.P4682F57 2008
741.5'973—dc22   2007032232

Summary: On April 10, 1912, fourteen-year-old Christopher Watkins boards the
Titanic with his mother and little brother. They are sailing across the Atlantic Ocean
to meet his father in the United States. Suddenly, the giant ship strikes an iceberg and
the unthinkable happens. The grandest ship ever built begins to sink! Christopher
must quickly become the man of the family and find a way to keep them safe.

Art Director: Heather Kindseth
Graphic Designer: Brann Garvey

Printed in the United States of America in Stevens Point, Wisconsin.
012011
006060R

TABLE OF CONTENTS

INTRODUCING . . .

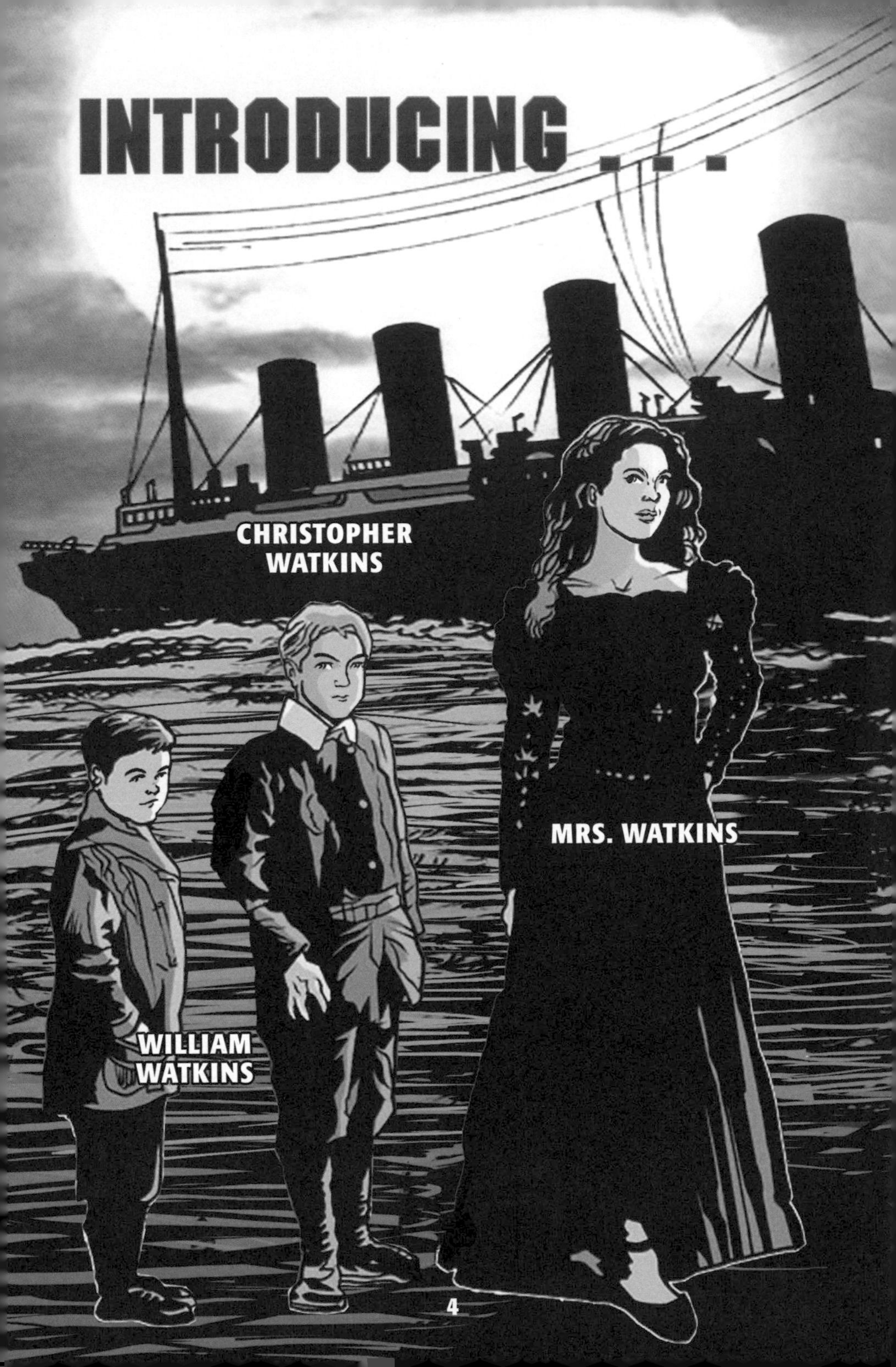
CHRISTOPHER
WATKINS
MRS. WATKINS
WILLIAM
WATKINS

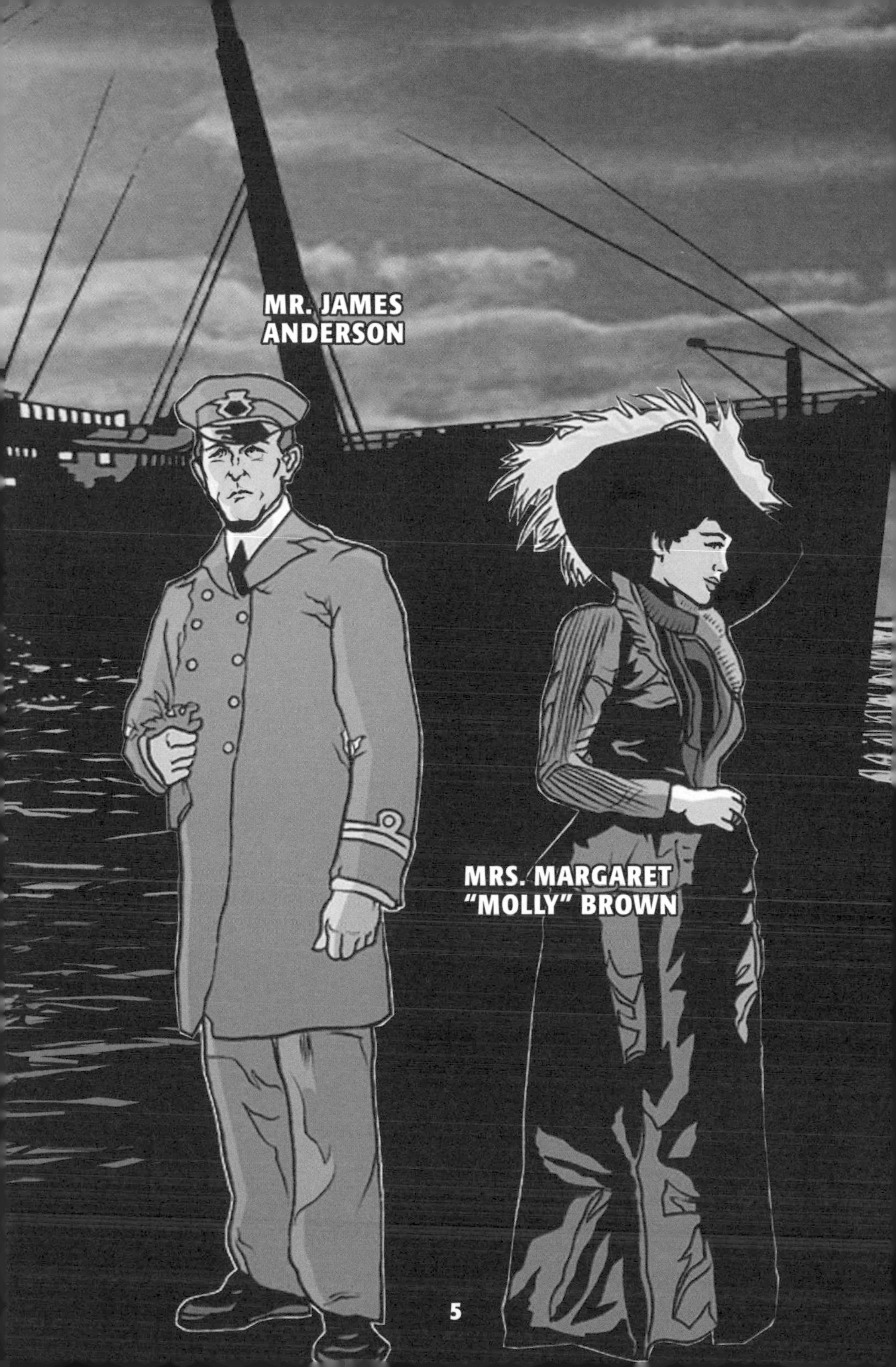
MR. JAMES ANDERSON
MRS. MARGARET "MOLLY" BROWN

Southampton, England, April 10, 1912.

Chapter 1

A GRAND VOYAGE

Christopher Watkins rounded a corner and stopped dead. There was the *Titanic*, the greatest steamship ever built.

Its four giant smokestacks soared into the blue sky. Its steel hull blocked the horizon. Flying atop the rear mast was the red flag of the White Star Line, the company that owned the giant ship.

That same red flag was printed on the ticket in Christopher's hand.

"I still can't believe we're sailing aboard her!" the twelve-year-old said. "And on the very first voyage, too!"

"Are you the Watkins family?" a man asked. "I'm James Anderson. I work on the *Titanic*. Mr. Watkins asked me to look out for you during your trip. Follow me, please."

Mr. Anderson led them to the gangplank for passengers in second class.

"She sure is big!" said nine-year-old William.

"The biggest ever," Christopher said. "She's 175 feet tall. That's as tall as 30 men standing on each other's shoulders!"

"She's 92 and a half feet wide," Christopher continued. "And 882 and a half feet long!

"She's got a swimming pool, a gymnasium, restaurants, two libraries, and even a post office!"

William's jaw dropped. "Did you hear that, Mother?"

Mrs. Watkins stepped onto the gangplank.

"You sure have a good memory, Christopher," she said. "But I don't care how great the newspapers say *Titanic* is. I just want to get to New York safely."

Christopher looked at his mother's worried face. He thought about the talk he'd had before his father left for America.

You are the man of the family until we're all together again, son.

Yes, Father. You can count on me.

Christopher took his mother's hand. "There's no need to worry, Mother," he said. "We'll be with Father in seven days.

Once on board, Mr. Anderson turned to Christopher. "You seem interested in the *Titanic*," he said. "Would you like to have a look below the decks and see what makes her go?"

Christopher smiled. "Would I ever! May I, Mother?"

Mrs. Watkins looked worried. "Is there any danger?" she asked.

"None at all," Mr. Anderson promised. "The boy will be with me at all times."

"Very well, then," Mrs. Watkins sighed.

Just then, the *Titanic's* three bronze whistles sounded. Moments later, the ship's engines came to life. Smoke blew out of three of the four smokestacks. Finally, the *Titanic* shook and started to edge away from the dock. Smaller ships blew their whistles as the *Titanic* gained speed and moved past them.

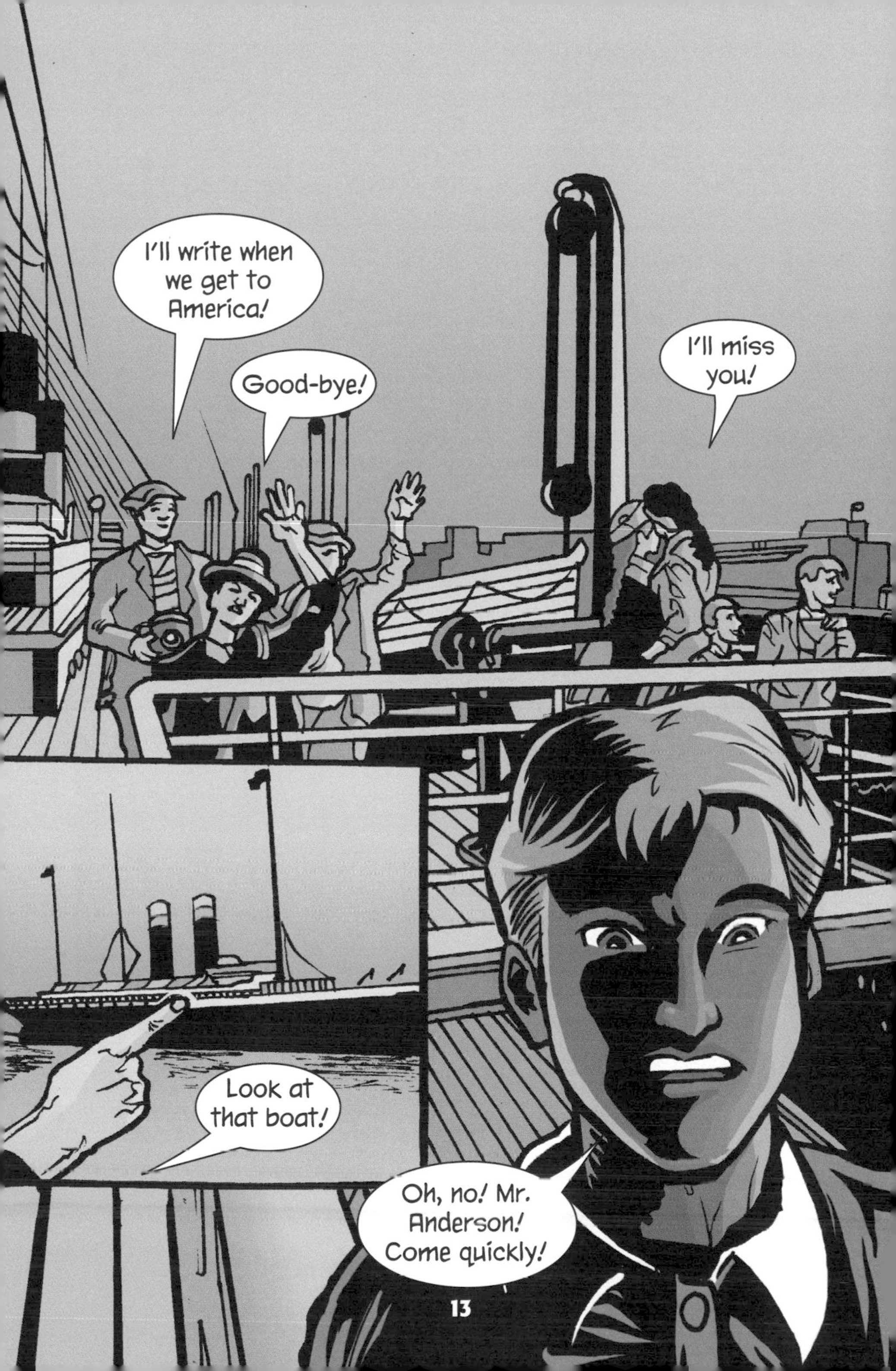
I'll write when we get to America!
Good-bye!
I'll miss you!
Look at that boat!
Oh, no! Mr. Anderson! Come quickly!

But the collision never came.

"Wh-what happened?" William asked in a shaky voice.

"We must have reversed in time," Mr. Anderson answered. He sounded relieved. "Look, here come the tugboats to steer the *New York* away from us."

"Come on, William," Christopher said. "We should check on Mother."

Mrs. Watkins's face was white. "What a terrible sign! We're not even out of port yet!" she said. "Thank goodness the *New York* didn't hit us!"

"Even if she had, nothing would've happened, Mother," Christopher said. "Everyone knows that the *Titanic* is unsinkable!"

Chapter 2

EXPLORING THE SHIP

As *Titanic* chugged across the English Channel, the Watkins found their room on E Deck. Later that afternoon, Mr. Anderson stopped by.

"We're docking outside of Cherbourg soon," he said, referring to a small French port. "That would be a good time to see the engines, if you still want to, Christopher."

"I sure do!" Christopher said, and then turned to William. "Do you want to come?"

William shook his head. "No, thanks. Mother said I could buy a souvenir before supper," said William.

"Just us then," said Mr. Anderson.

He led Christopher down some stairs and through a doorway marked "Passengers Are Not Allowed Beyond This Point." That door opened into the crewman's quarters.

They reached the bottom of the stairs. Engines shook the floor beneath their feet. The noise grew louder as they walked through a long hallway.

Mr. Anderson opened a large steel door and stepped back.

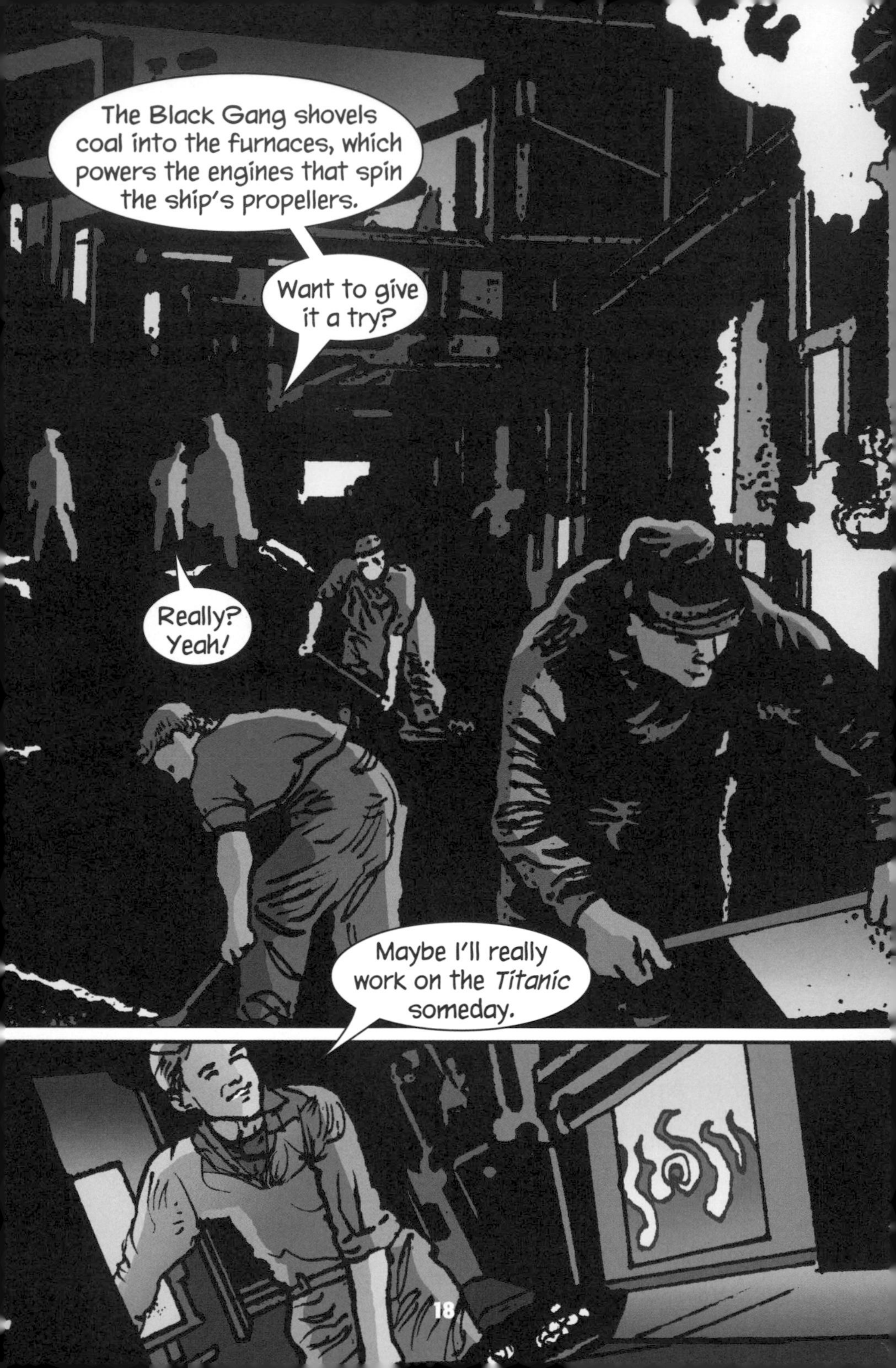
The Black Gang shovels coal into the furnaces, which powers the engines that spin the ship's propellers.
Want to give it a try?
Really? Yeah!
Maybe I'll really work on the *Titanic* someday.

Mr. Anderson took him to the engine room next. As they entered, Christopher heard a loud bell. Moments later, the engines slowed and then stopped.

"What's wrong?" Christopher asked.

Mr. Anderson pointed to a large dial.

"When they turn their dial upstairs, the one down here turns too," Mr. Anderson continued.

"So they ordered us to stop?" said Christopher.

Mr. Anderson nodded. "We must have reached Cherbourg," he said. "Time for you to head back to your cabin, Christopher. I have work to do."

The next morning, *Titanic* set out for the Atlantic Ocean. Christopher set out to explore other parts of the ship. William came with him this time.

The boys climbed the stairs past the dining room on D Deck. They reached the second-class library on C Deck and peeked in at the people reading or writing letters. They looked at each other, shook their heads, and continued on.

Outside the library was a deck where children were playing tag. William joined the game, but Christopher stared out at the dark water below.

That water must be freezing!

A few minutes later, he spotted a door with a sign: "First Class Passengers Only." He knew he shouldn't pass through that door since he was from second class. But he was curious.

The brothers pushed through the door and walked down the long hallway. At the end they found a beautiful staircase.

The Watkins boys climbed four flights of stairs. Then they reached the promenade deck, surrounded by first-class passengers.

"Chris, it's time to go!" William whispered nervously.

Christopher stuck his hands in his pockets and copied the stroll of the first-class men. "I told you before, no one cares if we're here!" he said.

The boys raced around a corner and nearly ran into a woman stepping out of an elevator. Christopher stopped just in time. Unfortunately, William didn't. He ran right into a lady.

Christopher's heart sank. No doubt the rich lady would turn them over to the crewmen. But to his amazement, the lady winked at him!

The boys didn't stop running until they'd reached their room. Then they fell onto Christopher's bed, laughing.

"That was close!" Christopher said.

William sat up. "Too close!" he said. "Think about what Mother would have said if we had gotten into trouble! Or Father!"

Christopher stopped laughing then. He'd forgotten his promise to his father!

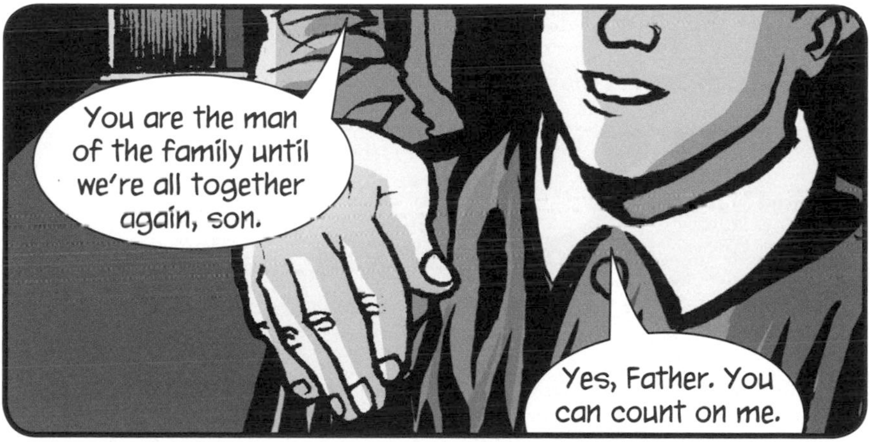
You are the man of the family until we're all together again, son.
Yes, Father. You can count on me.

Some man of the family I am, he thought. Well, from now on, I'll take that role seriously.

Chapter 3
COLLISION AT SEA

For the next three days, Christopher kept his promise. He looked after William and helped his mother. He wanted to see what the third-class section of *Titanic* looked like, but he didn't go. He knew his mother wouldn't want him there.

On April 14, the fourth day of their journey, Mr. Anderson took him to see the Marconi Room.

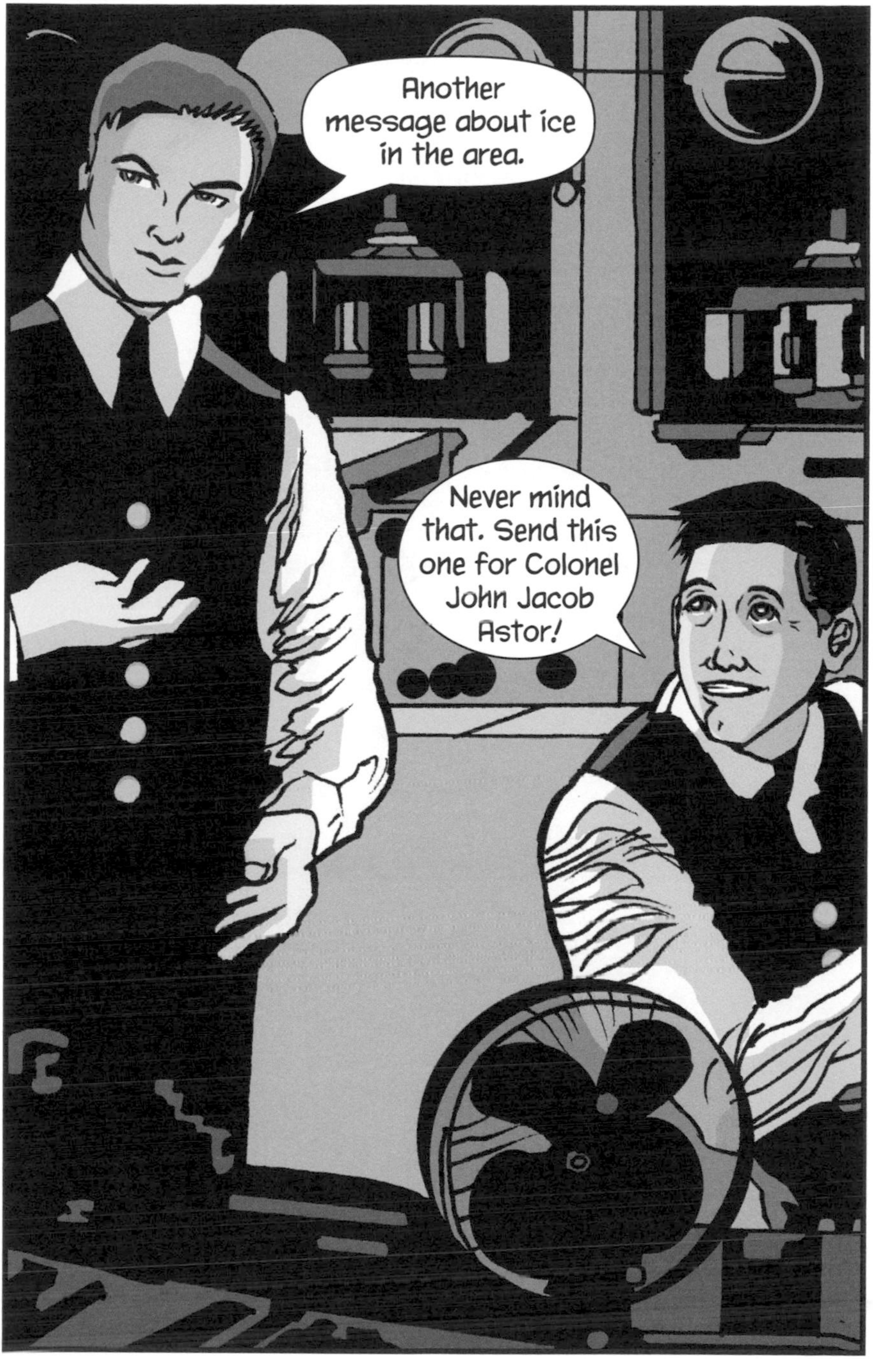
Another message about ice in the area.
Never mind that. Send this one for Colonel John Jacob Astor!

That night, Christopher dreamed of being the captain of an even bigger ship than *Titanic*.

Then suddenly, he was shaken awake!

His mother and brother were asleep. What had woken him? Had he heard something other than William's snores?

He listened for a minute more. Then he realized there was a sound he wasn't hearing. The engines had stopped.

Something has happened, Christopher thought. He swung out of bed, pulled on his clothes, and quietly left the cabin.

Cold air bit through Christopher's coat the moment he stepped onto the open deck. Stars dotted the black sky. He saw a row of lights moving on the horizon.

Another ship, he thought. Maybe we stopped to avoid crashing into her. But the other ship seemed too far away.

Christopher hoped to see someone who could tell him why *Titanic* had stopped her engines. Far down the deck, a group of men were laughing and kicking chunks of ice around.

Where did that ice come from? he wondered. He got an answer a moment later.

Christopher shivered again but not from the cold this time. An iceberg? That doesn't sound good, he thought.

It wasn't good. In fact, when the same officers returned minutes later, he learned that the situation was very bad.

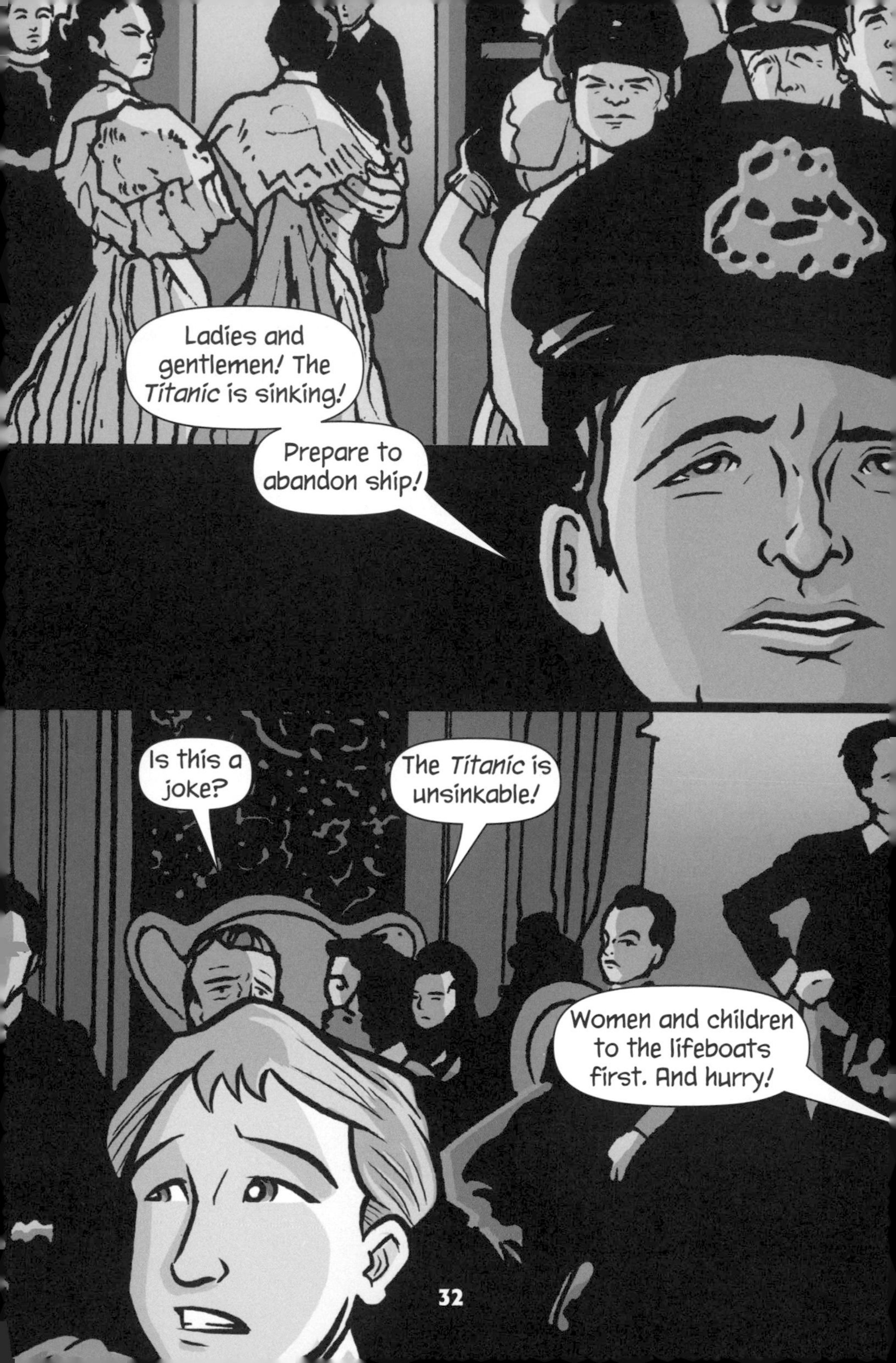
Ladies and gentlemen! The *Titanic* is sinking!
Prepare to abandon ship!
Is this a joke?
The *Titanic* is unsinkable!
Women and children to the lifeboats first. And hurry!

When Christopher heard that order, he knew the danger was real. William and Mother! he thought. They're still asleep in the cabin!

Heart pounding, he raced down three flights of stairs to E Deck. He pounded on every door he passed to wake up the passengers.

"Get up!" Christopher yelled. "The *Titanic* has hit an iceberg!"

Finally, he came to his own room and threw open the door. "Wake up! The *Titanic* is sinking! We must get to a lifeboat!"

He pulled William from his bunk and threw a pile of clothes at him.

Mrs. Watkins grabbed her bedding tightly. "I knew from the start that this ship was trouble!" she said, panicking. "We're doomed!"

Chapter 4
TO THE LIFEBOATS!

"We are not doomed," Christopher said. "Put this on." He held out her coat. "Please, Mother." Mrs. Watkins blinked back tears, but she took the coat.

The narrow hallway had been empty when Christopher had passed through minutes earlier. Now it was crowded with frightened passengers.

"William, Mother, take my hands!" Christopher called. "And don't let go!"

Christopher fought his way down the hall and up the stairs. After what seemed an endless journey, the family stepped onto the deck.

Christopher pushed his way through the crowd toward a lifeboat. Suddenly, William's hand was torn from his. Christopher searched around for his brother.

"Mother!" he cried. "Get in the lifeboat while I find William!"

With his mother safely aboard a lifeboat, Christopher ran off to find William.

Christopher found William. He tugged his brother to his feet and nearly carried him to the lifeboat. When William spotted their mother, he struggled free. He ran aboard the small craft.

Christopher moved to join them. Then he heard something that made him stop.

"Christopher!" Mr. Anderson ran up to his side. "Why aren't you in the lifeboat with your brother and mother?"

"I'm not sure I should," Christopher said. "My father —"

"Your father would want you to be on that boat," Mr. Anderson said. "These next hours will be full of danger. William and your mother will need your strength to see them through."

He pushed Christopher toward the small craft. "You must get into that lifeboat! Now!"

Christopher looked back at Mr. Anderson. "Will you come, too?" he asked.

"My duty is to help passengers into lifeboats, not to jump in one myself," Mr. Anderson said, shaking his head. "There's a crewman on your boat. He'll see to your safety."

The lifeboat gave a jolt. "Hold on!" the officer ordered.

Slowly, the boat started downward. As they slipped past the first deck, Christopher heard music.

"The ship's band is playing," his mother said.

The music faded as the lifeboat dropped lower. Finally, the boat hit the icy waves.

"To the oars!" the officer barked. "We must put distance between us and the *Titanic*."

"Shouldn't we help others?" a woman cried.

"When *Titanic* sinks," the officer growled, "she could drag us down with her!"

Christopher remembered how the *New York* had been pulled away from the dock. He began rowing with all his strength.

Christopher's shoulders burned. His palms stung and his arms ached. He didn't slow his strokes until he heard the order to stop. Then, he and the other survivors watched the death of the *Titanic*.

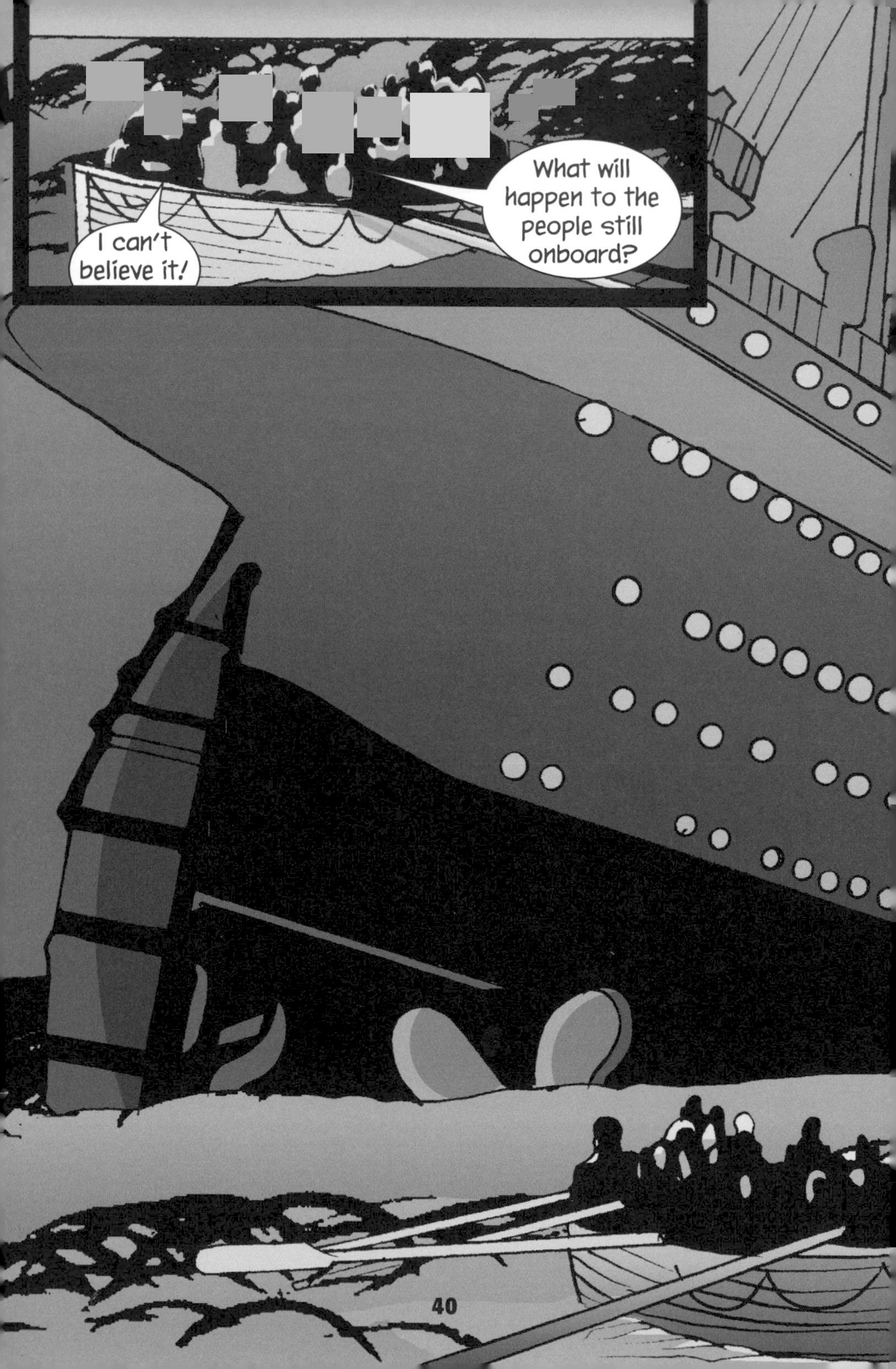
I can't believe it!
What will happen to the people still onboard?

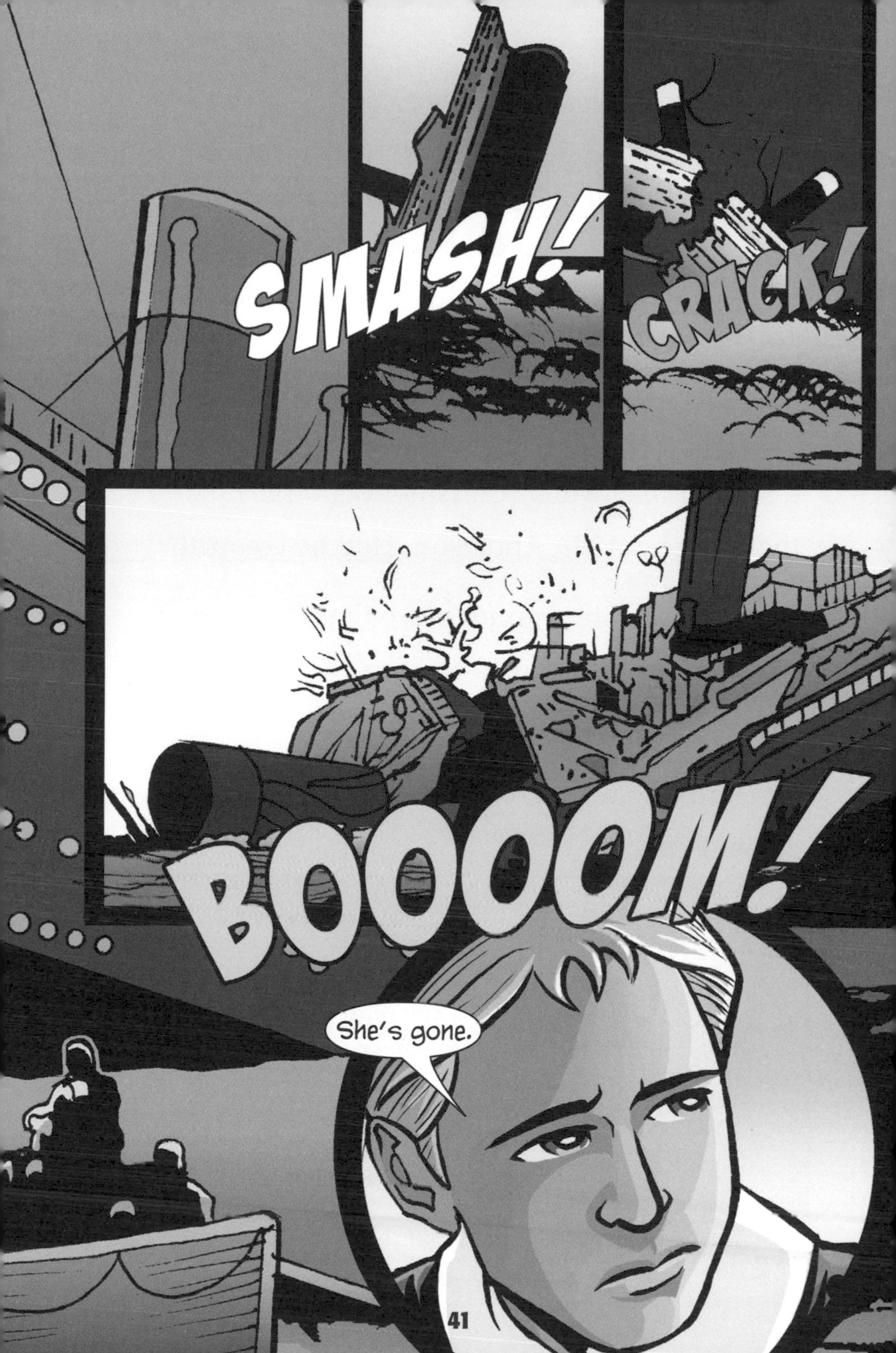
SMASH!
CRACK!
BOOOOM!
She's gone.

Chapter 5
RESCUE

All that was left of the unsinkable *Titanic* was a swirl of inky water. Christopher bit his lip and thought about Mr. Anderson. Had he escaped?

Suddenly, Christopher picked up his oar and placed it into the water.

"There may be survivors out there!" he cried. "We must go back and rescue them! Their lives depend on us!"

The officer cut him off. "Do you think the iceberg that sank the *Titanic* was the only one?" He shook his head. "If we go back, we put our own lives at risk. We can only hope that another ship heard our call or saw the flares."

As the minutes ticked into hours and no ship appeared, hope of a rescue was almost lost. People cried quietly and prayed out loud.

As the sun started to rise, Christopher looked at his mother. William was asleep in her arms.

"Christopher," she whispered. He moved beside her and took her icy fingers in his hand.

"We'll be all right, Mother," he said quietly. He rubbed her cold hands with his own and laid his head on her shoulder. "We'll be all right."

Even as he said the words, he wondered if they were true.

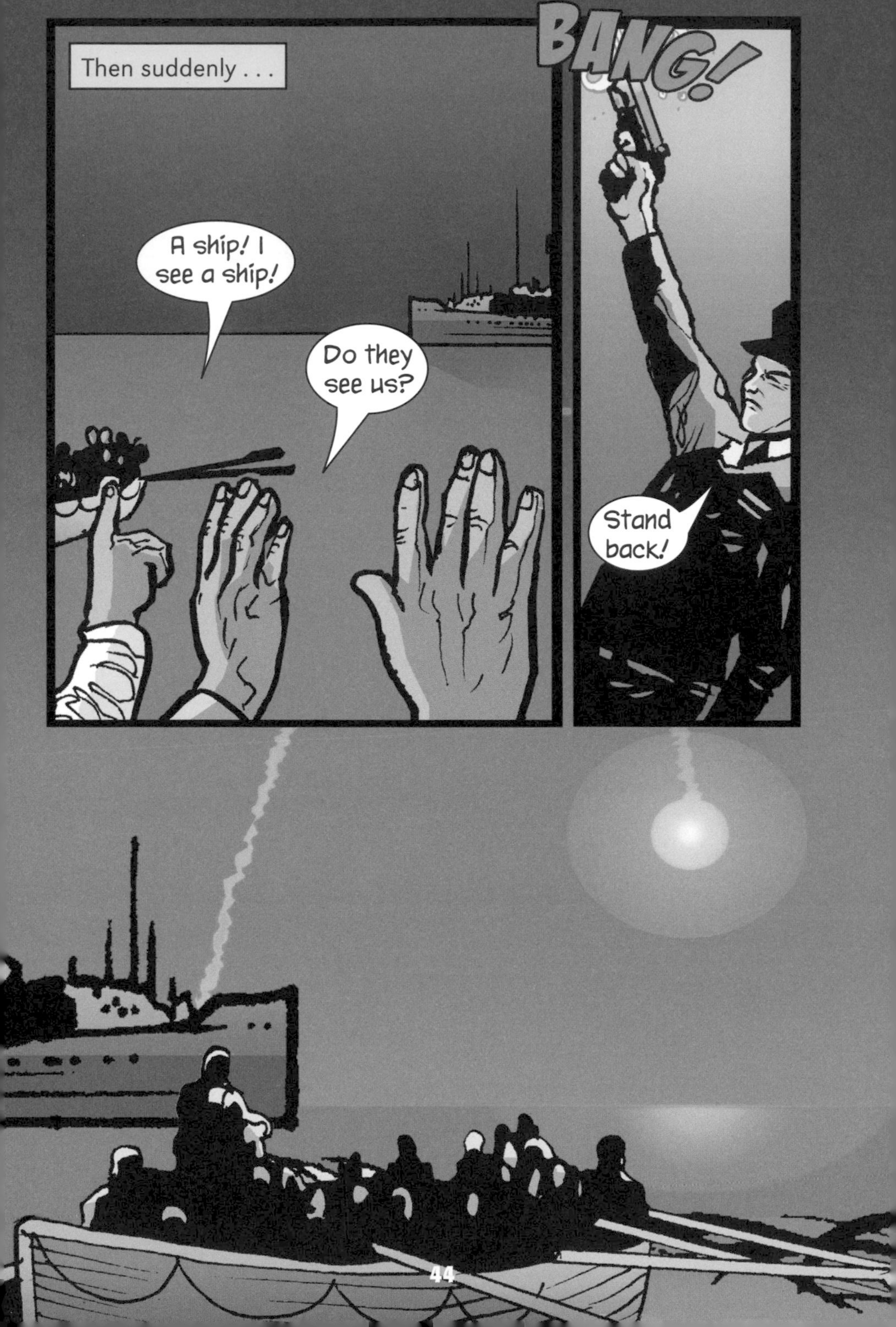
Then suddenly . . .
A ship! I see a ship!
Do they see us?
BANG!
Stand back!

Christopher's heart leapt. The ship was coming toward them!

"We're saved!" William cried.

The weary, frightened passengers shouted and waved as the ship drew closer. At last, it was right alongside them. *Carpathia*, her nameplate read.

"We're sending down ladders!" a sailor from the *Carpathia* shouted. "Those who have the strength to climb, use them to reach our deck! For those who are too weak or injured, we have slings to pull you up!"

"But you must all hurry!" he continued. "There are other lifeboats that need our help!"

The first rope ladders were tossed over the side. Three canvas slings followed. Christopher caught one and passed it to his mother.

"You're light enough for a sling," he said to her. "You go first. Then send it back for William."

Christopher watched as first his mother and then his brother moved up the side of the ship in the sling. Only when they had been pulled up to the *Carpathia*'s deck did he grasp a thick rope ladder. The scratchy fibers dug into his sore palms. He swallowed back a cry of pain.

I must make it to the top, he told himself.
He forced himself to climb. Christopher pulled
himself upward.

Just when he was certain he could go no further, strong arms grabbed hold of his coat and heaved him over the rail. He landed with a thud on the deck.

His mother bent over him. A tear slid down her cheek. "We are all safe," she whispered.

Christopher sat up slowly and stared out at the empty ocean. Somewhere far below the waves lay the wreck of the *Titanic*. He watched the sun begin to rise, still thinking of his mother's words and of Mr. Anderson.

Not all are safe, he thought. Not all.

ABOUT THE AUTHOR

After working more than 10 years as a children's book editor, Stephanie True Peters started writing books herself. She has since written 40 books, including the *New York Times* best seller *A Princess Primer: A Fairy Godmother's Guide to Being a Princess.* When not at her computer, Peters enjoys playing with her two children, hitting the gym, or working on home improvement projects with her patient and supportive husband, Daniel.

GLOSSARY

abandon (uh-BAN-duhn)—to leave somewhere or get off of something suddenly

gangplank (GANG-plank)—a small bridge leading onto a ship

grandest (GRAND-est)—the largest and most impressive of all

hull (HUHL)—the frame or body of a ship

port (PORT)—a place where boats anchor or dock

promenade (prom-uh-NAID)—a place for walking

souvenir (SOO-vuh-neer)—an object that someone keeps to remind them of a trip or event

telegraph dial (TEL-uh-graf DY-uhl)—a device for communicating between a ship's engine room and the room where the ship is steered

translate (TRANSS-layt)—to change a message from one language to another

tugboat (TUHG-boht)—a small, powerful boat used to tow larger ships

voyage (VOI-ihj)—a long journey, often by sea

MORE ABOUT
TITANIC

The RMS *Titanic* struck the iceberg at 11:40 p.m. on April 14, 1912. Two hours and 40 minutes later, the giant ship was gone. RMS stands for Royal Mail Ship. The *Titanic* was carrying mail, as well as passengers, from Great Britain to the United States.

At the time, *Titanic* carried 2,224 passengers. According to the United States Senate investigation report, 1,517 people died in the accident.

Mrs. Margaret "Molly" Brown was an actual first-class passenger aboard the *Titanic*. She helped many passengers find their way aboard lifeboats when the ship began to sink. Brown survived the disaster, earning her the nickname "The Unsinkable Molly Brown."

Lillian Gertrud Asplund, the last American survivor from *Titanic*, died at age 99 on May 6, 2006.

Titanic's final resting place on the ocean floor was a mystery for decades. On September 1, 1985, a research expedition led by Dr. Robert Ballard found the wreck. It was located 350 miles southeast of Newfoundland, Canada, 12,500 feet below the ocean's surface.

The wreck was too deep for humans to reach. Instead, Ballard and his team explored the sunken ship using special video equipment on remote controlled deep-sea probes named *Argo, Alvin,* and *Jason Junior.*

Today, hundreds of remains from the *Titanic* can be seen in museums around the world. These items include a trunk containing musical instruments, perfume bottles, dolls, and children's toys. More than 90 years later, these items still remind people of the many lives that were lost.

DISCUSSION QUESTIONS

1. Before the voyage, Christopher was excited about traveling aboard the *Titanic*. After what happened, do you think he would ever travel on a ship again? How could he overcome his fears?

2. Do you think Christopher's father would have been proud of the way he handled the situation? Explain your answer using examples from the story.

3. At the end of the story, Christopher is left wondering about Mr. Anderson's safety. Do you think Mr. Anderson escaped the sinking ship? Why or why not?

WRITING PROMPTS

1. Christopher had to face many fears to survive the sinking of the *Titanic*. Describe your biggest fear and how you've learned to deal with it.

2. Imagine you own a giant ship and write a high-seas adventure story. Where would you take your ship? What types of people would you meet? What problems would you run into?

3. This book has five chapters. Pretend you are the author and write one more. What happens next to Christopher and his family? The ending is up to you.

INTERNET SITES

Do you want to know more about subjects related to this book? Or are you interested in learning about other topics? Then check out FactHound, a fun, easy way to find Internet sites.

Our investigative staff has already sniffed out great sites for you!

Here's how to use FactHound:

1. Visit *www.facthound.com*

2. Select your grade level.

3. To learn more about subjects related to this book, type in the book's ISBN number: **9781434204448**.

4. Click the **Fetch It** button.

FactHound will fetch the best Internet sites for you.